*Growing*
# GREEN

# EATING
# LOCAL

## by Laura Perdew

LERNER PUBLICATIONS · MINNEAPOLIS

Copyright © 2016
by Lerner Publishing Group, Inc.

Content Consultant: Courtney Baines Smith, Department of
Sustainable Development, Appalachian State University, Boone, North Carolina

Lerner Publications Company
A division of Lerner Publishing Group, Inc.
241 First Avenue North
Minneapolis, MN 55401 USA

For reading levels and more information, look up this title at
www.lernerbooks.com.

**Library of Congress Cataloging-in-Publication Data**

The Cataloging-in-Publication Data for *Eating Local* is on file at the
Library of Congress.

ISBN 978-1-4677-9388-9 (lib. bdg.)
ISBN 978-1-4677-9711-5 (EB pdf)

Manufactured in the United States of America
1 – VP – 12/31/15

# Table of

# CONTENTS

# GROWING ROOTS

The football goalposts at Paul Quinn College in Dallas, Texas, rise above rows of fresh produce. Sweet potatoes are ready for picking on the twenty-yard line, and hens reside where the ticket booth used to be. Instead of fans cheering where the bleachers once stood, tilapia swim in large tanks. The local football field is now a farm.

After Michael Sorrell became president of the struggling college in 2007, he realized funding needed to be cut in some areas. He decided the football program should be one of them. Sorrell also realized that the school and surrounding community had limited access to nutritious, unprocessed foods, a problem that faces many urban and rural communities across the United States due to a lack of grocery stores or farmers' markets. Instead, people rely on convenience stores or fast food restaurants, which typically sell processed foods that are high in fat and sugar. In an attempt to bring healthier foods to the area, Sorrell tried to attract restaurants and grocery store chains to build on the unused football field. There weren't any takers. Then Sorrell proposed turning the football field into a farm, despite the fact

Schools around the world, including this one in Zimbabwe, are building and caring for gardens.

President Michael Sorrell started the We Over Me Farm at Paul Quinn College.

that the college didn't have an agricultural program and no one there really knew anything about farming.

Many people questioned Sorrell's vision. But Sorrell was determined. He eventually secured the necessary funding through a local philanthropist and PepsiCo. The We Over Me Farm started in March 2010. Since then, the entire 2.0-acre (0.8-hectare) football field has been converted into an organic farm that produces more than fifty different kinds of vegetables.

Four beehives, a chicken coop, a greenhouse, and a system for raising tilapia also populate the farm. Community volunteers and students in work-study programs cooperate to make the farm a success as well as a community gathering place.

Paul Quinn College serves farm produce in the school cafeteria and sells its products to local restaurants, grocery stores, farmers' markets, and even the Dallas Cowboys' stadium for concessions. Through donations, fundraising, and the sale of crops, the We Over Me Farm just about breaks even every year. But it is not satisfied with stopping there. As of 2015, the school had also secured funds to build both a grocery store and a restaurant—the first healthy food outlets in the area.

# A Short History of Food in the United States

What's happening at Paul Quinn College is part of a movement gaining force across the United States as more people seek out nutritious, fresh, and locally grown food. People want to know the farm or farmer who grew their produce or raised the cow that was the source for their milk or meat. And they want cooking and mindful eating to be reestablished at the center of US culture.

A mere one hundred years ago, everyone in the United States was a locavore, meaning they ate food that was produced nearby. In addition, most meals were cooked at home, and meals were eaten together with the family. There were no snack foods, no frozen foods, no commercially canned foods, and no national food brands. Then, beginning in the 1930s, road systems in the United States improved, creating the opportunity

In the early 1900s in the United States, families joined together to enjoy meals prepared with only local foods.

to transport food farther and farther from its source. Refrigerated trucks allowed food to be transported longer distances without spoiling. Farm technology also improved. Soon, small family farms were replaced by large-scale farms that operated similar to factories and corporations. At the same time, national and global food supply chains replaced local food supply chains.

As farm sizes grew, many farmers began producing single crops to sell, rather than the traditional mix of different crops to sell and to eat themselves. This monoculture food production allowed for single crops, such as corn and wheat, to be grown on a massive scale. Food processors also learned how to better preserve food, and food was increasingly packaged in boxes, cans, or bags. These processed foods were a boon for busy families looking for quick meals or snacks. By the 1970s, a majority of food production in the United States was industrialized. Family dinners were less the norm, and fast food restaurants and frozen dinners replaced fresh, home-cooked meals.

The industrialization of food production continued, including raising increasingly larger numbers of animals in close quarters. To stimulate milk production or growth, and to ward off diseases that plague farms where animals are closely confined, farmers began to regularly administer antibiotics, hormones, or other drugs, with undetermined health risks to humans. Farmers also began planting genetically modified seeds, also known as genetically modified organisms (GMOs), in the 1990s. By scientifically modifying organisms, scientists have created GMOs that are resistant to herbicides. This allows for a greater application of these weed-

To Your
HEALTH

## FOOD ON THE BRAIN

The industrialization of food processing made possible fast food restaurants and junk food. These food choices are extremely convenient, yet they are frequently high in fat, sugar, and salt and low in essential nutrients and vitamins. They are also addictive. Studies have shown that these ingredients stimulate the reward center of the brain in much the same way as many illegal drugs. As a result, the more fast food people eat, the more they crave it. Long-term diets based on fast food and junk food can lead to diabetes, high blood pressure, and high cholesterol, as well as obesity.

GMO tomatoes have been modified to stay firmer and have a longer shelf life than unmodified tomatoes.

controlling chemicals without damaging crops. Other GMOs have been engineered so that the crop itself releases a toxin as it grows. The toxin then repels insects. Scientific studies have yet to conclude whether GMOs are safe for human consumption.

The result of the industrialization of food production, GMOs, and the advent of processed foods is a dramatic shift in the types of food on grocery store shelves. Meat, milk, and eggs may come from animals treated with antibiotics or hormones. Other foods are full of preservatives and chemicals. And most processed foods are high in fat and sugar. This shift in food consumption in the United States has led to health concerns, including high rates of obesity, diabetes, and other diseases.

Modern food production has put the health of the environment and natural resources at risk as well. Not only is soil depleted by monoculture farming, but biodiversity, or the growing of a variety of plants, is also being lost in favor of single crops, such as corn and soy, that grow fast and resist pests. Water quality in rivers, lakes, estuaries, wetlands, and groundwater is also negatively affected by the runoff of chemicals used in commercial farming. In addition, the growing, packaging, and long-distance transportation of food in the United States accounts for 20 percent of the country's total fossil fuel consumption. This also accounts for substantial greenhouse gas emissions and air pollution.

## AVOIDING GMOs

As of 2015, the debate around the safety or risks of genetically modified food was ongoing and the scientific evidence unclear. Because of this, people looking to avoid GMOs do not eat processed foods that have corn, canola, or soy. They also avoid sugar because most of it doesn't come directly from sugarcane. Buying locally grown produce is another way to avoid GMOs, after getting to know a farmer's practices. Likewise, consumers looking to avoid GMOs should avoid meat from anonymous retailers because many animals raised for food are fed GMO corn, soy, and alfalfa.

As of 2015, identifying GMO products with a label was not required in the United States. Nevertheless, the Non-GMO Project, a nonprofit whose mission is to help shoppers make informed decisions, has created a seal that labels non-GMO products after going through a strict verification process. Consumers can also look for the "USDA Organic" label because food can only be certified as organic by the US Department of Agriculture (USDA) if it is grown and processed without GMOs.

# Locavores Unite

Confronted with these shifts in food production in the United States, some people are reconsidering the foods they eat and where that food comes from. Conversations about how food is produced and consumed in the United States, and the need for sustainable farming that will protect resources in order to feed both present and future generations, started as early as the 1960s. Yet it wasn't until the 1990s that people began to cultivate local food systems in large numbers. People started purchasing meat, fish, eggs, and produce directly from farmers. The number of supermarkets selling locally produced food increased. Schools across the United States are increasingly serving local food, as are hospitals and other institutions. Restaurants are also exploring new menus that feature local food.

So what exactly is local food? According to the 2008 US Farm Bill, the distance a product can travel and still be considered local is "less than 400 miles (640 kilometers) from its origin, or within the state in which it is produced." However, those involved with the local food movement—the farmers, market owners, activists, and consumers—generally define local as much more than simple geography. Yes, it is buying food grown in one's own town or region, but it also calls for shortening the supply chain instead of buying food from large retailers that get their food from anonymous, national suppliers. Likewise, local farms are generally smaller and use more sustainable practices than their industrial counterparts. Therefore, while not all local farms are certified organic, they tend to use organic farming practices, including preserving natural resources, avoiding GMOs, minimizing use of pesticides or herbicides, and supporting animal welfare. Local also means consumers get to know their farmer and his or her ethics, as well as the farmer's commitment to the community. And with the local food systems in place, and consumers and farmers reconnected, people can make more mindful decisions about food and unite around healthier bodies, communities, and the environment.

Between 1994 and 2013, the number of farmers' markets in the United States quadrupled.

# LOCAL FOOD SYSTEMS

One of the cornerstones of the local food movement is the mission to reduce the distance food travels from field to plate—otherwise known as food miles. The modern food industry ships the average food item 1,500 miles (2,400 km) from source to plate, whereas local food generally follows one of two much shorter supply chains: either direct to consumer or direct to retail. In the case of direct-to-consumer sales, meat, fish, and produce are sold directly by the farmer to the consumer. These methods include farmers' markets, community supported agriculture (CSA), farm stands or stores, and places where consumers can pick their own produce. Between 1997 and 2007, the profit of direct-to-consumer agricultural products increased 120 percent. Direct-to-retail methods, or food service, account for the majority of local food sales—five times more than direct-to-consumer methods. In this case, farmers sell their meat and produce to markets, grocery stores, restaurants, schools, or other institutions.

Do you know how far the packaged food you buy travels before it reaches your local market?

# Farmers' Markets

The idea of farmers' markets is not new—throughout history and across the globe, farmers have gathered to sell their produce in street markets

Farmers' markets are popular around the United States, from small towns to large cities. This market is in New York City.

# PLAN AND COOK A MEAL USING LOCAL FOOD

Make dinnertime family time at your house. As a family, pick at least one day of the week when everyone can commit to being home for dinner and plan the meal with an adult or sibling. Look through family cookbooks, or go online for healthy meal ideas that can incorporate local food. Then go shopping. How many of your ingredients can you buy locally at a farmers' market or co-op market? Does your local grocery store carry locally grown produce or meat? Avoid processed foods.

in Europe, the Middle East, and Asia. Yet in the United States, few farmers' markets existed before the 1990s. Farmers' markets are now found in cities and towns across the United States, and their numbers continue to grow. Farmers' markets are public places where farmers set up booths or tents to sell their meat, fish, eggs, and produce directly to consumers during the growing season. Farmers are usually charged a fee for the space in the market in which to set up a stand. Fresh fruits and vegetables make up the majority of sales at farmers' markets, followed by herbs and flowers. Meat is also sold at some farmers' markets.

At farmers' markets, consumers can wander through the venue and speak directly with the farmers. Farmers' markets have also become community gathering places where friends and neighbors meet to buy local foods, to socialize, and in some places, to watch live performances.

# CSAs

Community-supported agriculture programs (CSAs) are another form of direct-to-consumer sale. In CSAs, people sign up and pay to receive part of a farmer's crop. The idea of CSAs originated in Switzerland and Japan in the 1960s and was brought to the United States in the 1980s. In 1986, only two such systems existed in the United States. As of 2012, there were an estimated 6,500 across the country, with that number expected to grow.

Some farms allow CSA members to pick their own produce from the fields.

## Case In ✣ POINT

## LOCAL FISH

Commercial fishing is depleting our oceans at such a rate that some experts predict that 90 percent of the world's commercial fish will be gone by 2050. Moreover, 85 percent of the fish consumed in the United States is imported. Enter the local fish farmers to save not only the oceans, but also the US fishing industry. Across the country, local fishermen are reestablishing sustainable methods of fishing. Some have returned to hand-caught methods rather than commercial netting, which harvests great quantities of fish at a time, leading to overfishing. Others have begun community-supported fisheries, which operate similarly to CSA farms on land. They bring in different kinds of seafood, depending on the season, and provide customers with same-day-caught fish. There are also farmers who raise fish in large warehouses without chemicals or antibiotics.

To be part of a CSA, consumers purchase a share of the expected harvest from a farm at the beginning of the season. The cost to consumers is based on what a farmer expects to harvest, weighed against the cost of labor, planting, watering, harvesting, and the number of shares the farmer plans to sell. Some farmers also sell different sized shares or may offer discounts to those willing to provide labor on the farm. Then,

If crops fail due to weather or pest infestation, both CSA farmers and their customers share the risk, making it a joint effort.

throughout the season, customers pick up produce either at the farm or at a central location.

Consumers who buy shares in a CSA also take on some risk: shares are paid up front, and if a crop fails in some way, the weekly take-home basket may be only half full. Refunds are rarely given. This farm-share concept, though, helps build a sense that "we're in this together," and this attitude fosters a sense of community.

## Co-Op Markets and Grocery Stores

Farmers' co-ops are businesses owned and controlled by farmers. The first cooperative markets in the United States date back to colonial times, but it wasn't until the early 1900s that co-ops truly began to thrive. Then a new generation of co-ops started in the 1960s and 1970s. These stores led the way in the natural foods industry by selling whole and unprocessed foods.

Modern co-op markets are owned and run by members. This business system is based on values, such as community, health, and sustainability.

### FOOD AND FAMILY

One aspect of the local food movement involves bringing people together around food. This includes families. In the busy, modern world, families eat together much less than they used to. In fact, pediatrician Nadine Burke reports that 50 percent of meals are eaten outside the home (and 20 percent are eaten in cars!). She believes that eating at home is important because home-cooked meals are usually more nutritious, and families have more control over the ingredients that go into each meal. Eating at home also brings families together and gives members time to connect with one another. A growing body of research has revealed that families that eat together regularly are happier and healthier and have better relationships.

As such, co-ops work with local farmers to sell fresh produce, meat, and fish, most of which is grown using organic methods.

Large corporate markets are investing more in the local food movement as well. National retailers such as Whole Foods, Safeway, Kroger, Publix, and more have started local food initiatives. At some stores in Colorado, for example, locally grown produce is marked with a "Colorado Proud" label. This shift by larger chains is an effort to stay competitive as more consumers demand local food.

## Restaurants

Restaurants are going local too, and an increasing number of chefs are designing menus based on locally grown food. For restaurants, serving these farm-to-table meals has also become a marketing technique to bring in customers.

Restaurants that serve local food often purchase the food directly from farmers. In some cases, that means going out to the farm. In other instances, chefs visit farmers' markets to purchase food. This brings the freshest and highest-quality food to a diner's plate. Many restaurants even change menus daily or seasonally in order to serve only what is available from farms in their area.

## Schools

Lunches served in US school cafeterias are typically processed, high-fat, and high-salt foods reheated in microwave ovens. The local food movement is changing that too. The push for farm-to-school meals began in the 1990s as parents, teachers, and cafeteria staff recognized the need to improve

A "Colorado Proud" sign at this Walmart in Arvada, Colorado, lets consumers know their fresh produce is grown locally.

school lunch nutrition. The movement gained force, and by 2013, when the USDA conducted the first-ever Farm to School Census, they discovered that

Schools that connect with local farmers to supply cafeterias offer students the chance to try nutritious, fresh, local food.

more than 40,000 schools across the country served fresh, nutritious meals to more than 23 million students.

Numerous organizations nationwide are working together to continue connecting schools with local farmers, provide farm-to-school meals, and create school gardens. The hope is that these initiatives will create better eating habits and teach children where their food comes from. In addition to schools, other institutions are bringing local food to the table, such as hospitals and retirement facilities that incorporate local food into their cafeteria and patient menus.

## Case In 🌿 POINT
## ANN COOPER, THE RENEGADE LUNCH LADY

Ann Cooper, director of food services for the Boulder Valley School District in Boulder, Colorado, was once told that she couldn't put salad bars in schools because it's impractical. She didn't listen. Cooper has dedicated her life to providing healthy food and healthy food education to children. She knows that hungry and malnourished students have trouble learning and thinking in school. Despite naysayers, Cooper has made drastic changes in Boulder Valley's school lunch program. And even though the USDA says it's okay to serve French fries as a vegetable, Cooper doesn't. She doesn't serve chicken nuggets, chocolate milk, liquid cheese, or donuts, either. Instead, Cooper focuses on homemade meals using fresh, nutritious, and often local ingredients, including milk from Colorado cows, produce in salad bars, and homemade pizza. In schools that serve nutritious meals, reports indicate better academic performance and lower incidences of anxiety, absences, and behavior problems.

# 3

# BENEFITS OF LOCAL FOOD

**W**hy are so many people choosing to eat local? Because as local food systems grow stronger roots, people are seeing the health, environmental, economic, and social benefits.

A commitment to eating local food is, in part, a commitment to one's health. Not only is locally grown food fresher, better tasting, and unprocessed, but foods eaten soon after harvest retain more nutrients than those that are shipped long distances over many days or weeks. Likewise, processed foods that may be otherwise nutritious are depleted of vitamins, minerals, and other nutrients during processing. Local food systems can also encourage better food choices and healthy eating habits because of the availability of fresh, unprocessed foods.

Eating foods that are grown or raised locally also allows consumers to make informed choices about the food they eat. When buying local eggs, for example, consumers can visit the chickens to see how they are raised. They can talk to the farmer about their use of antibiotics. Consumers can also ask about the cows that provide meat or dairy, and whether they were

Eating local, just-picked fruits and vegetables ensures you're getting the most nutrients from your produce.

## SEASONAL VEGETABLES

Having fresh fruits and vegetables available all year is something that most Americans take for granted. Oftentimes, people don't consider or know the number of food miles their produce travels to reach their plates at all times of the year. Part of the local food movement is encouraging people to eat locally grown produce that's in season. If you're wondering what's in season in your area, go online and search for seasonal produce in your state. Then, see if you can plan a meal using only those fruits or vegetables. Many websites even have recipes you can follow. Can you go a week eating only in-season produce? A month? This may be easier in the spring, summer, and fall. Can you do it in the winter?

grass fed or grain fed. Studies have shown that beef from grass-fed cows is substantially more nutritious than grain-fed beef raised on factory farms. Nutrition benefits include less saturated fat; 75 percent more beneficial, essential fatty acids (omega-3s); 300 percent more vitamin E; 400 percent more vitamin A; and more minerals such as calcium, potassium, and magnesium. With respect to produce, consumers of local food can also talk to farmers about their use of pesticides, herbicides, or GMOs to determine if the produce is right for them.

## Food Safety

Another reason many choose local products is food safety. Farmers who raise and grow food for local markets are more invested in their relationship to consumers because the consumers are their neighbors, and they aim

Get to know the farmers in your area to find out where and how your fresh food is grown.

to provide them with healthy, safe food. Large agricultural businesses do not have the same personal responsibility to consumers. In fact, the industrialized food system in America sees regular recalls of food. This includes recalls for chicken contaminated with salmonella bacteria and prepared food found with *E. coli*. And while local farms do experience occasional problems, most health issues associated with food production are caused by the large scale of factory farming operations and attempts to cut costs. Further, the distribution chain of the industrialized food system is massive in both size and geography. Therefore, foodborne illnesses are difficult to track back to the source and contain as they spread.

Similar concerns about food safety surround food imported from other countries. The United States imports fresh fish, fruits, nuts, and tropical

## READ LABELS

While eating local, whole, healthful food is certainly important, it is not always practical. When buying prepackaged food, it's important to read labels in order to make informed choices about the food that goes into your body. Pediatrician Nadine Burke recommends starting with the number of servings per container, which gives you an idea of how much of something you can eat to get the listed calories, fat, sodium, and so on. She then says to look at the ingredients. The ingredient listed first is the most abundant in the food. The fewer ingredients in a food, the better. If high fructose corn syrup or sugar are named in the first five ingredients, you should avoid that food.

# SLOW FOOD MOVEMENT

In reaction to the ever-growing fast food industry, some people have come together around slow food. Slow Food is an international movement in 150 countries that seeks to preserve food culture, support local farmers and ranchers, and protect the environment. To do this, participants of the program sponsor events and activities such as food tastings or workshops to teach people about food and food culture. They share meals and advocate for policies that support local farmers in the face of the industrial food system. "Slow Food reminds us of the importance of knowing where our food comes from," said Alice Waters, vice president of Slow Food International. "When we understand the connection between the food on our table and the field where it grows, our everyday meals can anchor us to nature and the place where we live."

products not produced in the United States, such as coffee and spices. Due to consumer demand, food imports increased fourfold in the first part of the 2000s. As a result, the US Food and Drug Administration (FDA) was unable to keep up with inspections. Of the 200,000 shipments that came from China in 2006, fewer than 2 percent were sampled. Thus, consumers can't be assured that the food they are eating is safe. Local farmers, on the other hand, generally oversee most aspects of their operation, from farm to consumer or retailer, and thus are able to deliver safer products and also address potential problems.

# Environmental Benefits

Another reason the local food movement has gained momentum is because industrial farming focuses on growing single, high-yield, hardy crops that grow quickly, depend on chemical herbicides and pesticides, and withstand the long transport process. These practices, however, not only deplete the soil of vital nutrients and pollute water sources, but also contribute to a loss of diversity in the varieties of fruits and vegetables cultivated. In contrast, local food systems are more committed to environment preservation, which includes fostering biodiversity and rotating crops in order to maintain soil health, and minimizing chemical use. At the same time, protecting and supporting local farms also preserves green spaces from urban development.

Finally, producing and eating local food cuts down on greenhouse gas emissions. Eating locally reduces food miles, and because it's not processed and factory packaged, decreases emissions and fossil fuel consumption.

# Economic Benefits

In local food systems, farmers and communities see economic benefits because money spent in the community stays in the community. This has the potential to stimulate and sustain the economy of a region. When farmers sell directly to consumers or to retailers, they retain a greater portion of the profit because they've eliminated the steps in between. They no longer have to pay for another company to process, ship, distribute, and market their meat, fish, or produce. Local food also has the ability to stimulate nearby businesses. During farmers' markets, people are drawn to

Buying directly from a farmer benefits both the buyer and the consumer.

that area of the community. Studies show that people visit the market and
are then inspired to shop or eat at other businesses nearby.

## Food Security

Industrial food systems in America have evolved over time to feed a
growing population, and to allow for a variety of food products to be
available to consumers despite local growing seasons. Yet as sophisticated
as these systems are, their structure has nonetheless created food deserts.

Defined by the USDA, food deserts are "parts of the country vapid of
fresh fruit, vegetables, and other healthful whole foods, usually found in

Community and urban gardens are one way to bring fresh produce to food deserts.

impoverished areas. This is largely due to a lack of grocery stores, farmers' markets, and healthy food providers." In such communities, people can buy flip-flops and crayons at convenience stores but not affordable, nutritious food. The food that is available is processed and high in sugar or fat, or both, such as soda and chips. These communities are sometimes in urban areas, but they are also found in rural areas surrounded by farmland. The USDA reported that in 2008, more than 6.7 million homes had poor access to nutritious food.

In light of this, some people active in the local food movement are working to improve food security, which includes access to the right amount of food to live an active and healthy life. Efforts to promote greater food security include creating urban farms, farmers' markets, and outreach programs that attempt to bring healthful, fresh, and affordable food into food deserts. The goal, therefore, is to promote local food systems that will increase access to fresh, unprocessed foods.

# CHALLENGES TO THE LOCAL FOOD MOVEMENT

The local food movement grows stronger, and more and more people are taking action to improve their own health, as well as the health of the environment and their communities. While the benefits are numerous, the local food movement is not without challenges, and its future depends on how these challenges are met.

## Food Systems in America

One of the greatest obstacles to growing the local food movement is the current food system in the United States, which makes it more affordable for people to eat unhealthful foods rather than nutritious foods. This is a result of government subsidies to commercial agriculture, which keep yields high and costs low for crops such as corn, wheat, soybeans, and

Currently in the United States, it's often cheaper to buy processed, prepackaged food than it is to buy healthy, fresh produce.

## SCHOOL BUS FARMERS' MARKET

In many places around the country, people cannot get to a farm or farmers' market to buy fresh, local food. So Mark and Suzi Lilly, farmers in Richmond, Virginia, bring the farm to them. Using a converted school bus, Farm to Family distributes local food to urban areas. The school bus farmers' market carries local, seasonal products such as fresh meat, produce, dairy, and other homemade products, just as you would find at a street market. The Lillys also educate people about local food and healthful eating. Sometimes they even bring along farm animals so people can understand where their food comes from.

rice. Specialty crops, which are fresh fruits and vegetables, do not receive subsidies. Further, the subsidized crops are used to feed livestock raised for meat, dairy, and eggs, and are part of nearly all processed foods, which is, in part, what keeps the prices of these products low. Therefore, fresh fruits and vegetables are more expensive than processed, unhealthful foods. This means that struggling families can put more calories on their table by choosing unhealthful foods. For example, a family of four can spend three dollars to provide a peach for each family member. Or they could put the same amount of money toward boxed macaroni and cheese and get eighteen servings.

As a result, people claim that the local food movement is only for the wealthy. In order to address this, the US government has begun programs

Find out whether farmers' markets near you accept SNAP. If they don't, ask the organizers to consider joining the program so even more people can enjoy fresh, local food.

that connect low-income families with fresh food. One such program is called the Supplemental Nutrition Assistance Program, or SNAP. SNAP provides a system through which low-income individuals can purchase food at some farmers' markets. There is also the Farmers Market Nutrition Program (FMNP), which offers extra money to seniors and low-income mothers so they may purchase food from local farmers. Likewise, some farmers have sought to address this issue on their farms. In an attempt to make local food available to all, some CSAs offer reduced-price shares to low-income families or participate in SNAP.

Yet even for families that want to make healthy food choices and are willing to pay for it, having access to nutritious food is sometimes a challenge. In both rural and urban areas, low-income families have been greatly affected by the loss of small farms and local restaurants, as well as the consolidation of the food process into a large, national system. The resulting food deserts force families to rely on what is available nearby. These options are generally fast food restaurants and convenience stores— places that traditionally do not sell fresh produce.

To Your
**HEALTH**

## TRY SOMETHING NEW

In the world of industrial agriculture, most people expect their apples to be red, their potatoes to be white, and their carrots and pumpkins to be orange. Yet one stroll through a farmers' market or on a local farm will reveal that these items come in a rainbow of colors. Did you know that potatoes can be purple? Local food sources also offer produce not typically seen in traditional grocery stores, such as kumquats or kohlrabi, depending on where you live. Simply browse the stands at a farmers' market to find something new to try.

## STORING WINTER CROPS

One of the great challenges of going local for consumers is having a supply of produce all year round. Something you can do at home is store winter crops for eating during the nongrowing season. Potatoes are an example of a winter vegetable that stores well in a cool, damp place, such as a basement. Winter squash, sweet potatoes, onions, and garlic also store well in cool places, but these veggies like drier places. Another great source of produce in the winter is root vegetables, such as carrots and beets. Before the growing season ends in your area, talk to a farmer, perhaps at a farmers' market. They will have additional information about what to store and how best to store it.

# The Culture of Food

Prepackaged, processed, and fast foods have not only forced many low-income families to make unhealthy food choices for the sake of cost, but have similarly created a predominant cultural expectation in America that food should be convenient as well as cheap. This includes snacks at the ready, dinners that can be prepared in minutes, and fast food restaurants in every community. One in four meals eaten in the United States is fast food.

Even consumers interested in eating healthy are accustomed to eating a wide variety of produce despite the growing season. Local food advocates encourage people to eat seasonally despite how difficult this may be in some areas of the country. For most Americans, this would mean giving up fruits such as bananas and oranges. Canning or freezing fruits and vegetables that do grow locally to eat out of season are possible solutions, but these take planning and time. Even eating locally in season demands an investment in planning and time, as home-cooked meals are much more labor intensive than grabbing a burger on the go. Yet the local food movement is also promoting the social benefits of gathering around preparing and eating food.

And while convincing people to cook from scratch at home is challenging, convincing school districts to do it in their cafeterias is an even greater challenge, despite the fact that well-nourished children do better in school. In addition to financing the purchase of local food, which is more expensive than federally subsidized meals, school lunch programs interested in implementing farm-to-school programs must also find the resources to finance the purchase and installation of new equipment, and they must train staff to actually cook instead of merely reheating packaged meals.

## The Farms Themselves

Farms and farmers are the core of the local food movement. As such, they are also at the epicenter of the challenges facing the movement. To begin with, the amount of usable farmland in the United States continues to decrease as populations increase. At the same time, the number of people to feed keeps increasing. In addition, farmers made up less than 1 percent of the US population in 2007. With so few people working in agriculture,

In the United States and around the world, growing populations are encroaching on farmland.

industrialized farming practices are the only way to produce enough food for everyone. There is debate, then, about whether small-scale, local farms can feed the masses. Advocates of industrial farming argue that this would be impossible. Yet there is a growing counter-argument that industrial farming itself uses too many resources and is too dependent on fossil fuels and chemicals to continue into the future. The alternative, they argue, is agriculture that is environmentally sustainable and can meet demand by placing less stress on resources and working in harmony with people and the environment.

These smaller, local farms, however, face the challenge of finding the right balance between scale and efficiency to turn a profit. In addition, because small farms do not have the large infrastructure and money of industrial farms, they are more affected by crop failures, pest infestations, and weather than corporate farms. They also cannot invest in large marketing campaigns. Likewise, small-scale farmers are up against their larger competitors when it comes to food safety regulations. While the

## SIMPLE, HEALTHFUL FOODS

Food journalist Michael Pollan asserts that the recipe for eating healthy has been overcomplicated in recent decades by food pyramids, nutritionists, and food marketers. In fact, eating healthy is actually quite simple, according to Pollan: "Eat food, not too much, mostly plants." Pollan also suggests avoiding processed foods, especially those with high fructose corn syrup and anything with more than five ingredients. This is where local food plays such an important role. Visiting farmers' markets or taking part in CSAs allows consumers to follow Pollan's advice and to choose fresh, nutritious produce, meat, dairy, eggs, fish, and more.

Eat local to help support small-scale farmers in your community.

safety measures required by the 2011 Food Safety and Modernization Act
have reduced the number of foodborne illnesses and deaths in the United
States, they do not differentiate between large- and small-scale farms.
The central problems for small farms are the overwhelming amount of

Advocates are banding together to expand the local eating movement.

paperwork and new farm infrastructure required by the act. For example, while regular testing for *E. coli* bacteria in water seems reasonable and even beneficial, complying with the regulation is more difficult for small farm operations because the testing and recording systems cost far more than their operating budgets allow. Local farmers contend that they already have a contract with consumers as well as a vested interest in selling safe food.

While there are certainly challenges facing the local food movement, people at the heart of the movement embrace the value of local food on every level and are willing to take on these challenges. It is the farmers, consumers, chefs, school cafeteria staff, and other advocates with a passion for local food who will sustain the movement into the coming decades.

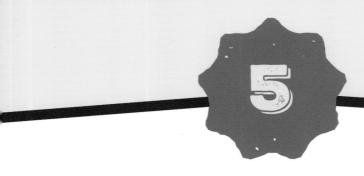

# THE FUTURE OF LOCAL FOOD

I nterest in local food is growing, yet the future of the local food movement in the United States will depend on redefining the food system, as well as changing the steps local farmers take to efficiently produce, market, and distribute their food.

## New Infrastructure

Since small, local farms simply do not have the efficiency level of industrial farms, local food activists across the country are seeking ways to make their small farms more efficient and more profitable. To do this, they are building new infrastructure that connects the small farms in different ways. One networking practice that will carry local farming into the future is creating food hubs that can collect and distribute local farm products, making them more accessible. In Virginia, the Local Food Hub does just that. Instead of fifty different farmers making twenty of their own deliveries to retailers, the Hub collects and delivers the food. This saves farmers time and gas, and consumers reap the benefits of accessible, local food.

Fall Line Farms, a food hub, lets buyers order online from dozens of Virginia farms and pick up their food in one place.

As another example, in the western United States, ranchers have formed a co-op group that raises beef sustainably, humanely, and profitably. For the ranchers, this allows for shared marketing efforts. Working together, they can provide a year-round supply of beef to a large customer base, which is something individual small ranches wouldn't be able to do on their own. Not only does this co-op business model allow local ranchers to make a living, it also supports local communities. The future of such ranches and small-scale farms will rely, in part, on their ability to join forces to meet demand.

# Spreading the Word

Spreading the word about local food is important to the movement's success. One way local food activists do this is through farm-to-school initiatives. These programs are changing the way kids think about food, and

Students in San Diego, California, choose from foods provided locally through the Farm to School and Healthy School Meals organization.

studies have shown that kids are actually consuming more fresh produce than the USDA recommends. By educating youth, the local food movement is creating markets both now and in the future. Likewise, the more restaurants that incorporate local food in their menus and highlight the farms food comes from, the more people will become aware of the benefits of local food.

Local farmers must also connect to community markets in order to create demand. Marketing strategies include advertising, building relationships with community members interested in local food, and exploring the possibilities for new markets. One specific way to increase demand is for farmers or local food advocates to create a local food guide

## Case In 🌿 POINT
### CHIPOTLE RESTAURANTS

One of the new business models for local food is localizing fast food. On the leading edge of this trend is Chipotle Mexican Grill. Owner and founder Steve Ells believes that it is important for people to know where their food comes from. To that end, Ells has dedicated himself and his restaurant to sourcing the food locally, attempting to buy organic whenever possible, buying meat that was raised with respect, and avoiding GMOs. And while the food at Chipotle may cost a bit more than traditional fast food, he believes that the quality of food and the restaurant's mission are what keep people coming back.

Bill Niman of Niman Ranch in California supplies humanely-raised meat to Chipotle.

that outlines the benefits of local food and where consumers can find it. Planning and developing farmers' markets is another way to grow the market for local food. Some community groups have created bumper

By organizing farmers' markets, small, local farmers can make more profit on direct-to-consumer sales.

stickers with catchy slogans, published regional food maps, promoted farm tours, developed harvest festivals, and more.

## A New Generation of Farmers

As the local food movement continues to grow and the demand increases, supply must increase as well. The future success of local food depends on creating new farmers. Many organizations are working to make this possible, including helping new farmers find suitable farmland and acquire necessary skills. Today's farmers need to know a lot more than how to raise a cow or create a farm system. They also need to know how to run a business. The new generation of farmers will need to fully understand the economics of farming, learning to think like a business owner as well as a farmer in order to find a profit.

New farmers also need financial support to find land, buy equipment, and build a business. Traditional groups, such as the Farm Bureau and Future Farmers of America (FFA), have supported and strengthened agricultural communities for decades. New groups have also emerged to assist the new generation of farmers. The National Young Farmers Coalition, founded in 2009, helps new farmers tackle the many challenges they face when starting a farm business. Realizing that all young farmers

To Your
HEALTH

## EAT A RAINBOW

As part of the movement to get kids to eat healthful foods, schools are also inviting students to eat a rainbow. In the Boulder Valley School District in Boulder, Colorado, for example, students are challenged to create a rainbow of fruits and vegetables from the cafeteria salad bar, selecting a fruit or vegetable for each color of the rainbow. These Rainbow Days encourage kids to try a variety of produce they may be unfamiliar with while at the same time teaching them about healthy food choices.

FFA helps prepare new generations of farmers for agricultural leadership.

face the same issues, the founders realized that if people worked together, they would be better able to fight for the future of independent and sustainable farming.

## WAYS TO GO LOCAL

Becoming part of the local food movement starts with a single step. To support local food, there are many things that individuals can do:

- Visit a farmers' market and talk to the farmers.
- Go to a farm and see where local food comes from.
- Plan a meal using foods you can find locally.
- Visit websites to find sources of local food in your area.
- Volunteer at a community garden, school garden, or with other local food programs.
- Join a CSA.
- Try locally grown produce you've never tasted.
- Find out what produce grows seasonally in your region.
- Plant your own garden.

# Agriculture Technology New and Old

The new generation of farmers is also finding that running a farm requires not only boots that can get muddy and a reliable tractor, but also a computer. Cutting-edge software programs help farmers streamline the business side of farming, making production, marketing, and distribution much more efficient. Different technology solutions include software to manage a CSA or to track flock and egg production for independent egg producers; software to operate food hubs and co-ops; programs to assist in delivering food; and much more. The Internet is also a tremendously helpful

New technology, such as drones, is playing a role in helping farmers monitor and raise their crops.

tool young farmers use to market their food, create online marketplaces, and establish valuable networks.

Agricultural technology is also evolving. For example, farmers can fly drones to survey and photograph land and gather data. Information the drones collect is downloaded in the form of a report. The drones can be used regularly to help farmers see how crops grow and change over time, helping farmers manage water better, improve farming practices, and monitor crops.

Not all current farming practices are new, however, and the key to many local farms is integrating traditional methods into their practices. This includes using natural solutions for pest control, enforcing scientific practices to improve soil quality, and making use of the sun's energy for cooling and heating in greenhouses. This also includes creating complex farm ecosystems so that each aspect of the farm—animals, plants, soil, and water—are interdependent just as in natural ecosystems.

It is on these small, sustainable farms that the future of the local food movement rests, even in the shadow of industrial agriculture. Local food advocates believe that the future of the movement also means a better future for individuals, communities, and the environment. Accordingly, they hope that people from all across the country will continue to have food experiences, small and large, good and bad, that will educate and resonate with them, and move them to seek out local food. It is these moments, and the steps of individuals, that will keep the roots of the local food movement growing.

## Working as a
# LOCAL FARMER

**W**hen Anne and Paul Cure started a small farm near Boulder, they knew that they were making a lifestyle choice. They knew that their days on the farm would be dictated by the needs of the animals, the weather, and the demands of the changing seasons.

Since making that decision in 2005, they have created a farm ecosystem that supports natural diversity and sustainability. On their 12 acres (5 hectares) of land, they not only grow more than 100 varieties of herbs, vegetables, and flowers but also raise ducks and chickens for eggs and pigs for meat. They even have bees. Everything the Cures raise and produce is distributed within 50 miles (80 km) of the farm. The farm itself is a CSA, and they have a farm store on the property. They also participate in local farmers' markets and sell to local restaurants.

The Cures work the farm themselves, along with a small staff and seasonal interns. Through the internships, the Cures help promote small-scale, sustainable farming for the next generation and offer valuable hands-on experience to future farmers.

# GLOSSARY

**farmers' co-op:** a business owned and controlled by farmers

**infrastructure:** the basic equipment and structures needed for an organization to function properly

**local food:** food produced, processed, and distributed within a particular geographic boundary.

**monoculture farming:** the cultivation of a single crop over a large area and period of time

**organic:** food that is grown without the use of pesticides, fertilizers, or other chemicals, and without the addition of any preservatives

**processed food:** food that is packaged in boxes, cans, or bags

**subsidies:** government financial support to crop producers

# SOURCE NOTES

**13.** Steve Martinez, et al., "Local Food Systems: Concepts, Impacts, and Issues, ERR 97," *U.S. Department of Agriculture, Economic Research Service* (2010), http://www.ers.usda.gov/media/122868/err97_1_.pdf.

**31.** "About Us," *Slow Food USA*, https://www.slowfoodusa.org/about-us.

**33.** Mari Gallagher, "USDA Defines Food Deserts," *American Nutrition Association*, http://americannutritionassociation.org/newsletter/usda-defines-food-deserts.

**44.** "Michael Pollan, 'Real vs. Fake Food,'" *Nourish: Food + Community*, http://www.nourishlife.org/2013/12/real-vs-fake-food/.

# SELECTED BIBLIOGRAPHY

Auge, Karen, "Spoiled System: Eating Healthier Comes with a Price for Families," *Denver Post*, September 5, 2010, http://www.denverpost.com/ci_15996357.

Cobb, Tanya Denckla. *Reclaiming Our Food*. North Adams, MA: Storey Publishing, 2011.

"Co-Op – Stronger Together," *National Co+Op Grocers*, http://strongertogether.coop/.

Gayeton, Douglas. *Local: The New Face of Food and Farming in America*. New York: HarperCollins, 2014.

Gustafson, Katherine. *Change Comes to Dinner: How Vertical Farmers, Urban Growers, and other Innovators are Revolutionizing how America Eats*. New York: St. Martin's Griffin, 2012.

*Ingredients: The Local Food Movement Takes Root*. Dir. Robert Bates. Optic Nerve Productions, LLC, 2009. Film.

# FURTHER INFORMATION

Barker, David. *Organic Foods*. Minneapolis, MN: Lerner, 2016. Read more about what is considered organic and how you can eat organically.

Flounders, Anne. *Growing Good Food*. South Egremont, MA: Red Chair Press, 2014. Learn where food comes from, the growth of CSAs, and how your choices about the foods you eat affect your health and the environment.

The Lexicon of Sustainability
http://www.lexiconofsustainability.com/short-films/#
Watch videos to learn more about ways you can be a more responsible, sustainable consumer.

Nourish
http://www.nourishlife.org
Read and view dozens of articles and short videos from individuals at the forefront of the conversation about food, health, and sustainability.

Roberts, Jack L. *Organic Agriculture: Protecting Our Food Supply or Chasing Imaginary Risks?* Minneapolis, MN: Twenty-First Century Books, 2012. Learn more about organic agriculture, including information about pesticides and GMOs.

Seasonal Food Guide
http://www.sustainabletable.org/seasonalguide/seasonalfoodguide.php
Type in your state and the month to find out what produce is in season. Then, find some new favorite recipes!

10 Steps to Becoming a Locavore
http://www.pbs.org/now/shows/344/locavore.html
Read more about ways you can become a locavore and support your community.

# INDEX

## Photo Acknowledgments

The images in this book are used with the permission of: © Jeffrey M. Frank/Shutterstock Images, p. 1; © SuSanA Secretariat/CC2.0, p. 5; © David Pellerin/AP Images, p. 6; © Russell Lee/U.S. Farm Security Administration/Office of War/Library of Congress, p. 8; © Gabrielle Hovey/Shutterstock Images, p. 10; © ChameleonsEye/Shutterstock Images, p. 13; © Pavel Ilyukhin/Shutterstock Images, p. 15; © Jay Lazarin/iStockphoto, p. 16; © Tom Wang/ Shutterstock Images, p. 18; © Evlakhov Valeriy/Shutterstock Images, p. 19; © Olaf Speier/ Shutterstock Images, p. 20; © Kathryn Scott Osler/The Denver Post/Getty Images, p. 23; © Steve Debenport/iStockphoto, pp. 24, 46; © Hiroshi Teshigawara/Shutterstock Images, p. 27; © monkeybusinessimages/iStockphoto, p. 29; © Alex Milan Tracy/Sipa USA/Newscom, p. 30; © Peter Bernik/Shutterstock Images, p. 33; © littleny/Shutterstock Images, p. 34; © Niloo/ Shutterstock Images, p. 37; © Richard B. Levine/Newscom, p. 39; © Peter Zijlstra/Shutterstock Images, p. 41; © grafxart8888/iStockphoto, p. 43; © auremar/Shutterstock Images, p. 45; © Lance Cheung/USDA, p. 49; © Mike Blake/Reuters/Newscom, p. 51; © Craig Lee/San Francisco Chronicle/Corbis, p. 53; © Joe Bielawa/CC2.0, p. 54; © Kenny Kemp/Charleston Gazette/AP Images, p. 56; © Robert Mandel/Shutterstock Images, p. 58.

Front cover: © iStockphoto.com/Steve Debenport (top left); © A.L. Spangler/Shutterstock.com (top right); © Jeffery M. Frank/Shutterstock.com (bottom left); © Peter Bernik/Shutterstock. com (bottom right).